Hey, It's Me, Walter.

By Dianne Kowal Kirtley

Sketches by Colleen Kirtley Eckert

"Hey, It's Me, Walter," by Dianne Kowal Kirtley. ISBN 978-1-947532-07-6 (softcover); 978-1-947532-08-3 (eBook).

Published 2017 by Virtualbookworm.com Publishing Inc., P.O. Box 9949, College Station, TX 77842, US. ©2017, Dianne Kowal Kirtley.

Hi, everyone. I'm Walter.

Yeah, I know, weird name for someone like me, but it's the one I came with when I was brought to the shelter. I don't remember much before that day, but I think someone really loved me because I'm a very happy guy.

Life in the shelter was nice and safe, but a little confining, and I kept hoping that somebody might take me to a different place where I could do a little more exploring. One day I saw Mom and Dad come and give me the once over. I liked the way they looked at me, and I especially liked the fact that they smelled real good.

When they took me out of my cage, I knew we were definitely a match.

Mom said, "Oh, he's so cute. He is definitely the one."

Dad said, "Well, I guess he can't make too much of a mess." (Wrong about that one, Dad.) "But, he seems very sweet.

And I think his name is definitely a winner." (Okay, that's when I knew this guy and I were on the same page.)

Life is great at my new place. I still have a cage for sleeping and when Mom and Dad go to someplace called work. But when they are home, I have so many great places to run and chase balls and hide and go up and downstairs. Whew! I get tired just thinking about it.

Some of Mom and Dad's friends have stopped by to meet me and they pretty much say I'm one of the cutest dogs they've ever seen. I may be taking just a bit of liberty there, but that's usually the gist of it.

"Look at that sweet beagle face. And those cute little basset legs. Does he have the beagle bark?"

Beagle bark, let me see, I'll give it a try. "Arf, arf," I muster in my best voice.

"Yeah, well, don't let him see the full moon, or you might hear something else."

I guess I'll worry about that comment when I get a little older.

Everything was going just fine until I heard Dad say one day that I was going to spend a day at Grandma's.

"Grandma's," I wondered. Is that a farm or track someplace where I could really give these legs a workout?

I saw Dad putting my cage in the car, and all I could think was, "Oh, oh, now I've done it." Honest, Mom, I'm so sorry about those fake flowers I munched up, and, I know, the shoe that tasted so good and I just couldn't resist was your favorite. Please, please, I'll try to do better.

Dad grabbed me and put me in the cage, and I was really worried for a while but then I just got so tired and fell asleep. Even in the car, my cage feels really safe.

"Okay, Walter, we're here. This is Grandma's."

Well, the outside of this place looks okay, but you never know. I heard someone say that you can't tell a book by its cover. Now, I have no idea what that means, but it seems the right thing to say.

We went through the door, and suddenly I wasn't so worried: the smells were really great and explore, wow, you just can't imagine. I immediately took a right turn and decided to run upstairs.

"Hey, you little mighty mite, not so fast. We're going to stay on this level for a while."

I think I have heard that voice before, but I can't quite place it.

I heard Dad's voice say, "Okay, Mom, we should be home around six. We probably won't even stay for the whole game."

They left! OMG! I sat at the door for a few minutes or so, well, maybe seconds or so. No, really a few micro seconds or so.

"Well, little man, it's just you and I. And I've got a lot to do today, so you'll stay out of mischief, won't you?"

Little man? Well, first of all, I'm a dog, okay a guy dog, but stay out of trouble? That's an area that I cannot make any promises about.

I decide to give that upstairs another go, but man, this person really moves pretty fast for someone who's called grandma. We go from one bedroom to the next and she closes the doors as I make a quick sniff before she slams them shut. At the last one, I see that great, big BED, and I exert all my energy and make it up.

"Hey, little scallywag, get down from there. Dogs don't belong on beds."

Really? Whose rule is that? Sounds pretty silly to me. So, I give myself another boost and up I go.

"Walter, I said no beds. Now come on, there are plenty of other places to go?"

Not as soft as this, lady.

"I said, get down, Walter."

Now this sounds serious. Her voice is a bit more stern, and I'm beginning to see a test of wills here. I decide to give it one more try, and up I go.

"Alright, little guy, that's enough."

    I retort with a few sturdy barks, but let's face it. I'm not up to an out and out confrontation. Sometimes discretion is the better part of valor. Again, I'm not sure where that idea comes from, but it seems to fit here. I concede round one and roll over on my back.

    "Oh, you little cutie," she says.

    I knew it. She obliges by scratching my tummy.

I see another interesting place in this room and up I go. Suddenly, I'm adrift on the sea, my legs are weak and I'm feeling dizzy. This thing I'm on just goes back and forth, back and forth. I'm too afraid to jump off.

"Oh, oh," she says. "Is that rocker just a bit too much for you?"

She seems back on my side again, but why is she laughing.

BEEP! BEEP! BEEP!

Forgetting the rocker problem, I quickly jump off and we both race downstairs to investigate this horrible noise that has just assaulted my ears. I expect to see flames breaking out any second now.

"Okay, little guy, don't get scared. It's just the timer on the oven."

Whew! That's a relief, even though I have no idea what that means, but Grandma's voice tells me we don't have a problem here.

"Back up now, Walter, while I open the oven to check on the cake. It's going to be hot in there. Well, I guess you'll just have to learn first-hand."

I know she has tried to warn me about something, but I really like to stay in the mix of things. Suddenly, she opens this big box called an oven, and WOW, it's really hot and my nose feels as if it is on fire. I do the swift back-step when danger appears.

"I told you," she says. "Grandmas really do know more than dogs, you know."

Okay, point made, granny, but let's not get condescending about it.

"Now, as soon as I finish icing this cake we'll be going for a walk."

WALK! WALK!

It's the magic word. It means running and chasing and SMELLING the most wonderful outside things in the whole world.

I stay real close to Grandma's heels for a while, at least fifteen seconds, but she seems to have forgotten about the walk. I guess I'll just do a little more exploring.

I try the sun porch. Oh, man, how did I miss this stuff before. There are some new toys on the floor, little soft thingies that are just great for carrying in my mouth. Shall we take a tour of things, boys?

"What is that you have in your mouth, Walter? Oh, no, not the little penguin stuffed toy. I should have collected those before you came. Why don't you play with your own toys?"

Is she serious? BORING! New stuff is always more interesting. Okay, though, Penguin is off-limits.

This icing-business is really taking a lot of Grandma's time. I think I'll explore the den. Why didn't I see this room before? Just a little hop up and, whoa, watch it, it's almost another one of those rocker things, but not quite as bad. Steady, there, old boy. Okay, let's see ...Kleenex, newspaper and this red stick here. Yep, let's try the red. Now, real quiet, we'll just sneak past the kitchen and run into this other room and hide under this nice big whatever. Just a couple of munches here, yes, it feels really good on these new choppers.

"Walter, where are you? What's that noise? Oh, no, not Grandpa's red pen! He uses that to check his Sudoku."

Okay, okay, lady. I have no idea what his Sudoku is, but I hope it isn't painful when he gets up in the morning.   The red pen was a little too hard anyway. I need something just a little bit softer ....

I sneak away to the den again. (You know, being this short, can actually have its advantages.) This time I find a soft, but not too soft, square thing, and oh, yes, gnawing on this corner is just delightful. I'm trying very hard not to be noisy this time because this whatchamacallit is so perfect.

"Walter, where are you?"

Quiet, quiet, melt into the scenery...no munching...

"There you are! Oh no, not the coaster. Good grief, Walter, isn't there a minute when you cannot chew or get into something."

Well, there's the rub, you see. I happen to be a five-month old puppy.

"Alright, I guess it's time for that walk."

OKAY, finally! Let's do it.

The only problem with the walk is that I have to wear this darn harness. To tell the truth, I feel like a total dork with this thing on. First of all, it's awkward to put it on. I have to let my legs be grabbed and put into the slot and then it gets buckled on, and really, can't I just be relied on to walk beside Mom or Dad or this Grandma person and be trusted? Well, there it is, the answer is, unfortunately, a big fat NO.

And, we're off. I love it! New smells! The grass on my feet.

"Stay on the sidewalk, Walter."

Are you kidding? Doesn't feel anywhere as nice as that soft, moist grass. However, this fella is just not getting a chance since Grandma seems to rein in my leash every time I venture a little too far into the lawns.

Nonetheless, I love it. I have to moan a little bit to make life interesting.

"Walter, can't you just walk in a straight line."

I am. It's called a straight, zigzag, follow your nose path. And let's GET GOING! Why is she walking so slowly? C'mon, c'mon, follow me!

"Walter, slow down a bit. We've got a few miles to go this morning, so we need to pace ourselves.

Pace? A word unknown to my extensive vocabulary. I continue to PULLLL at that leash because I'm sure she'll start running a little bit. That's what Mom and Dad always do.

But I have to admit these new smells are great! This is a block I've never walked before, so, of course, I make my obligatory marks by lifting my leg at about every six feet.

"It really is a mystery to me how dogs always have enough urine to last an entire walk."

Yes, definitely, one of the great mysteries of the universe. Also, does anyone know what "urine" is?

Grandma has picked up the pace a bit, thank Heavens. I thought we might be out here all day. That wouldn't be so bad, except a fella tends to get a bit thirsty once in a while. In fact, you don't happen to see any hose running or a puddle of nice, cloudy water that I could have a drink from, do you?

I must be slipping because I didn't see these two approaching us. I think I'll try a big, old bark at this mammoth black dog and the leash holder just to make a statement. But something isn't quite right. We all stop and I do a little sniffing, but the dog's face is so grey, and when he moves, his legs don't move easily, his steps are slow, and his face looks pained. Suddenly I have a very sad feeling come over me. His face looks familiar, like someone I saw before with a grey face and legs that hurt to move and someone saying, "You know, Dad, you can't manage Walter anymore."

And then that grey face is gone forever, and I wake up in a cage in a new place.

"Look out, Walter, we've got two bikes coming at us."

Whew, I must be slipping, these two dudes almost wiped me out.

"Can we stop and pet the puppy?" It's one of the bike guys asking the question.

"No, Jack, we have to get home. Dad said only an hour at the park."

Spoil sport. I like when people stop to pet me. They always say the nicest things about the "cute puppy," yours truly, of course.

But here comes another group and I can tell right now that they are definitely going to do some heavy petting. It's a group of the talls with the minis. That's the name I've given to the little people, who are only about two or three times taller than I am. They always smell the best, though at my height you have to be wary of the occasional eye-poker in the group.

"Can we pet your dog, lady?" one of the taller minis asks.

"Of course, Walter is very friendly."

That's the reward for good behavior.

With just a little hop, I manage to lick the face of one of the minis, and he begins to cry.

Oh, oh, now I've blown it.

"Walter, don't jump up, you'll scare the children, especially the littlest one.

Sorry, kiddo, just couldn't squelch my enthusiasm. So I decide to settle for second best. I start licking their fingers, which are definitely a treat. Yum, yum, I hit the trifecta, with three of my favorites: applesauce, old cookies and dirt. Anyone have a drink of water to wash these treats down?

"Well, we've got to get going now," says one of the talls. "Say goodbye to Walter."

"Bye, bye, Walter. We hope to see you soon."

You bet, mini, and I'll bring one of my official fan club badges.

Across the street two poodle types are doing their best hotsy-totsy walk . Do you believe it? I'll think I'll just give them my fiercest bark.

ARF! ARF! ARF!

(think real loud.)

What? Not even a head turn? Are you kidding? Hey, it's me, Walter. You know, cute, adorable, petable, all of the above.

Stuck ups! You know, some characters are just too snooty for their own good.

A few more blocks, a few more turns, and I realize we have been out for about six hours or so and my tongue is nearly touching the ground.

"What? How come you're dragging now, Walter? What happened to all that zip and verve you had at the beginning of the walk? Not too far, just a few last blocks up the hill."

I knew it. This granny, sadist character has saved the biggest challenge for the end.

"Okay, this is it. We're home. You don't want to go any farther, do you?"

Right, a real comedian this grandma is.

"Well, hopefully, that might have tired you out and you'll take a little nap."

What can I say? Two gallons of water and a few small treats have revived me and I'm ready to go.

Grandma sits down in the kitchen and I decide to join her on a nearby chair. But what's this? With my front paws on the seat of the chair, I suddenly start moving. Help! Help! I can't let go here and my back legs can't move that fast. Who the heck has chairs that roll, for Pete's sake, and on this wood floor?

I hear Grandma laughing and she finally rescues me from my dilemma, picks me up, and sits me in her lap. That's okay for a few seconds, but, let's face it, there are just too many places in this house to discover. I squirm my way out of her lap and with a mighty jump, I'm back in explorer mode.

I have simply lost track of time and achievements, with all the running and smelling and chasing and "Walters, where are you?" but I think the scoreboard could be as follows:

Walter

Two artificial plants, leaves, stuffing, whatevers
Munched two gnarled coasters of carpet material,
corners gnawed
Two mauled stuffed toys, Penguin and Wolfie
(used to howl when squeezed)
One small puddle on kitchen floor (all that water,
you know)
A formerly usable red pen
Various tissues and Kleenex, shredded, before the
bathroom door was unceremoniously shut

Grandma

One flop of a cake despite pounds of icing

Just when I think I could really be in some serious trouble, they're back! It's Mom and Dad!

I just missed you both so much I can't stop running. It's just been terrible here. Please, please, don't ever leave me here again!

"So, Mom, how did it go? We didn't stay for the whole game because we thought you might need to be relieved."

"Well, he is really cute, but he's definitely high maintenance," replies Grandma.

High maintenance? Has granny here seen the length of my legs? And, I'm not deaf, you know, just vertically challenged.

After Dad packs up the car, we're on our way, and I've been such a good boy that I get to sit in Mom's lap in the front seat.

"Now remember, hon, no crazy driving. We don't want to jostle Walter."

That's right, Dad. Remember that there's a BABY ON BOARD. (can't help myself, just love that line)

It's just a short ride home, especially when a nap comes into play, but we make a stop during the trip, and then I hear the voices of some minis near us at a stop light. We're just a few feet away from their car, and I pop my head up to get a better look into their vehicle.

There's a girl mini in the back seat, who is looking directly at me. I give her the ole tongue-hanging-out smile, and when she talks, her squeaky little voice makes my head cock a bit, which I've learned, always works to my advantage. So, head cock and then ...wait for it, wait for it ....

"Oh, he's so cute, Mommy. Can we have a puppy like that someday?"

"Well, we'll just have to see, but only if you can be really good."

That's right, little girl, you be very, very good and pray real hard, and maybe, just maybe, you might be able to have a puppy *almost* as cute as me, Walter.

CPSIA information can be obtained
at www.ICGtesting.com
Printed in the USA
LVOW05s0419010917
547171LV00022B/210/P